EGMONT

We bring stories to life

First published in Great Britain 2012
by Egmont UK Limited
239 Kensington High Street, London W8 6SA

Editor: Catherine Such • Art Editor: Amanda Hartley
Designers: Kerrie Lockyer, Gary Knight, Kelly-Anne Levey
Editorial Assistant: Hannah Greenfield
Group Editor: Kate Graham • Group Art Editor: Jeanette Ryall

ISBN 978 1 4052 6331 3
51512/1
Printed in Italy

All this inside ...

DISNEY · PIXAR Cars 2

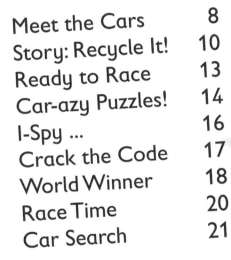

DISNEY · PIXAR MONSTERS, INC.

FINDING NEMO

TOY STORY

WALL·E

Answers Page 67 ▶

Meet the Cars

Read on to download lots of information about your favourite Cars characters.

Mater ▶

Lightning's best friend from Radiator Springs, Mater is a rusty tow truck with a heart of gold.

⬙ Lightning McQueen

Racing car Lightning McQueen is fast and famous. He'd love to win the World Grand Prix.

8

Holley Shiftwell ♥

Holley is a young secret agent on her first mission. She has lots of high-tech weapons and gadgets.

● Professor Z

An evil weapons designer, Professor Z is determined to ruin the World Grand Prix.

Colour
Colour the star next to your favourite character.

● Finn McMissile

British secret agent Finn McMissile is daring and brave. He'll stop at nothing to catch the bad guys.

DISNEP · PIXAR
Cars 2

Recycle It!

SCREEECH

1 Lightning was practising at the racetrack. He had an important competition coming up soon. "Excellent time, champ!" Sheriff praised.

"Pit stop!" said Guido. Lightning was practising so much, his tyres kept getting worn down! Poor Guido was running out of space to put everything.

ZZWEEEEEEE

2 Just then, Sally arrived. "How are the trials going?" she asked. "Great, thanks!" Lightning replied. "But I have to keep replacing my tyres!"

3 Lizzie overheard Lightning. "I can recycle those tyres," she said. "Do you know what to do with paper, too?" Lightning asked. "I sure do," replied Lizzie.

Point to Lightning's headlights.

4 Lightning took Lizzie to the Rust-eze Pavilion. "We keep all the stuff we don't use anymore in this warehouse," he explained. "Wow!" gasped Lizzie.

5 Lizzie spotted some poster boards. "I can help you get rid of these, too," she said. "Can you autograph them with your tread mark?" "Sure!" said Lighting.

6 Lightning couldn't understand why Lizzie wanted him to autograph everything, but he did it anyway. "Here's another one!" she shouted.

A little while later, Lizzie was ready to go. "What a load!" said Lightning. "It's a good thing you've got Sarge to lend a wheel!" "Where to?" asked Sarge.

11

Car-azy Puzzles!

How quickly can you help the cars complete these exciting activities?

M

T

R

A

E

Top Secret ▶

Holley is in on a secret assignment. Copy the letters below into their matching coloured circles to discover who she's meeting.

Picture Puzzle ▶

Follow the keyboard lead and guess whose picture has been scrambled.

14

Who is it? ▷

Join the dots to reveal a speedy Cars character!

Odd One Out ▷

Which picture of Raoul is the odd one out?

a

b

c

I-Spy...

Mater has spied some car close-ups.
Help him work out who they are!

Clue
Look at pages 8 and 9 to help you!

Write the name underneath each picture.

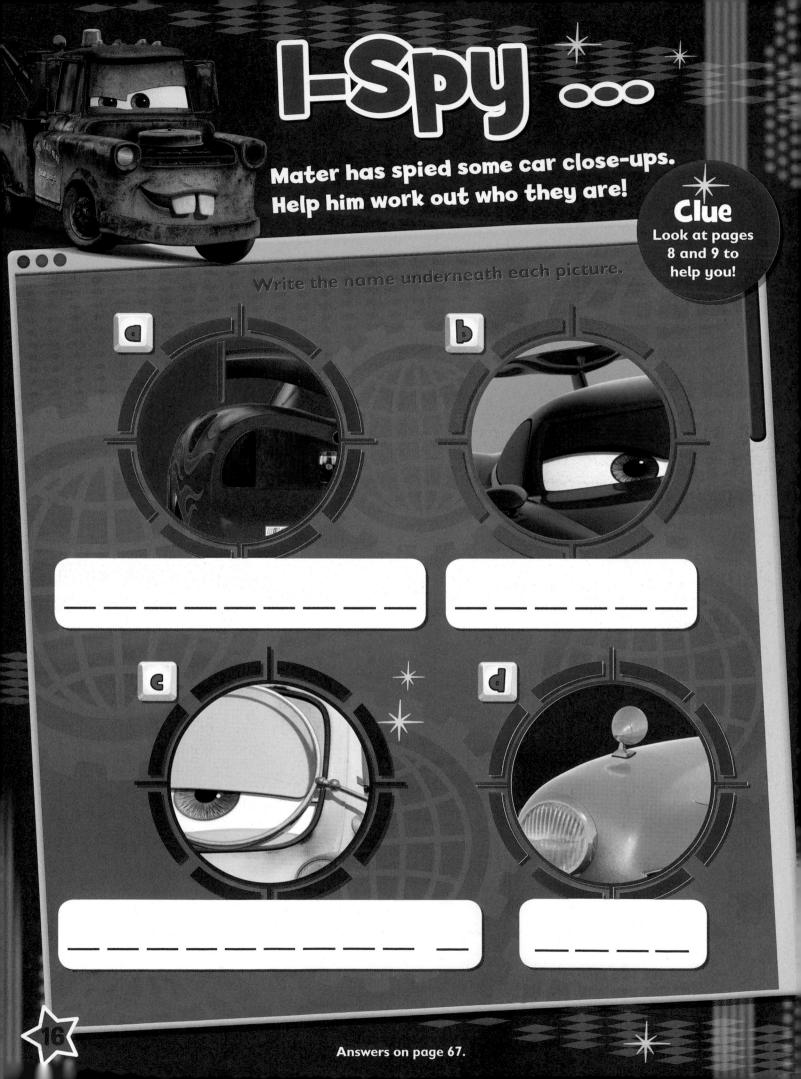

a

b

_____

_____

c

d

_____

_____

Crack the Code

Can you help Finn uncover the top secret destination?

Use the grid to help work out where Professor Z is hiding.

	a	b	c	d
1	L	G	I	C
2	P	W	R	N
3	O	J	Q	T
4	A	B	D	X

Hint
We've found the first letter for you.

a,1   a,3   d,2   c,4   a,3   d,2

L

Answer on page 67.

17

World Winner

The cars are lined up and raring to go.
Who will win the World Grand Prix?

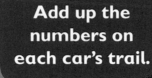
Add up the
numbers on
each car's trail.

Lightning ①

Francesco ①

Max ①

Raoul ①

③

②

③

①

③

18

Winner
The one with the highest total is the winner.

Car Clues ▶

Can you work out who's talking to Lightning? Follow the clues!

1 He's not blue!

2 He's bigger than Luigi!

3 He has both headlights!

Race Time

The cars are racing in Tokyo. Can you spot five differences in picture b?

a

b

Colour
Colour a cup as you spot each difference.

Answers on page 67.

Car Search

Can you find the names of the cars below hidden in this wordsearch?

Hint! Names go across and down.

HOLLEY

FRANCESCO

PROFESSOR Z

ACER

GREM

LIGHTNING

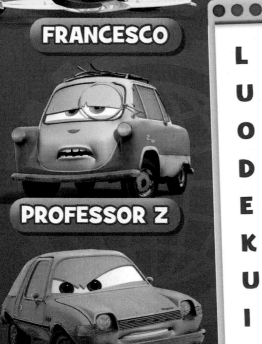

L	P	H	O	L	L	E	Y	O	X	L
U	R	K	S	M	U	P	C	F	S	I
O	O	R	O	A	A	S	J	R	F	G
D	F	P	C	T	E	T	C	A	W	H
E	E	L	I	E	S	R	E	N	Q	T
K	S	F	N	R	T	E	V	C	K	N
U	S	A	I	R	Y	T	F	E	Q	I
I	O	A	I	S	F	Q	R	S	O	N
F	R	U	K	T	I	X	N	C	R	G
U	Z	G	H	U	N	Q	J	O	J	P
R	I	V	K	N	N	K	G	R	E	M
A	C	E	R	C	V	R	H	H	G	N

FINN

MATER

Answers on page 67.

21

Monster Action

The residents of Monstropolis come in all shapes and sizes. Scroll down to find out more ...

Randall

Randall is a sneaky monster. He can make himself invisible by blending into the background.

Mike

Funny monster Mike is Sulley's best friend. He's always telling jokes and having lots of fun.

Celia

Snake-haired receptionist Celia is sweet and kind. No wonder Mike has a soft spot for her!

Mr Waternoose

Mr Waternoose is the head of Monsters, Inc. He's a crab-like monster with lots of eyes.

Colour
Colour the star next to your favourite character.

Sulley

Big, furry Sulley is the top scarer at Monsters, Inc. He takes his job very seriously.

Boo

Boo may be small, but she's very brave .... no monster can scare her!

The Frozen Roar

1 It was a cold morning in Monstropolis and Sulley and Mike were going to work. Suddenly, Mike giggled and threw a snowball at Sulley.

"You want a fight?" laughed Sulley. They pelted each other with snow. It was great fun! "We'd better get going now or we'll be late," chuckled Mike.

2 Later at Monsters, Inc., Mike got their first door ready. But Sulley's fur was wet and his throat was sore. "I'm getting a cold," he sniffled.

3 Sulley dashed through the door and into a boy's room, ready to scare. He tried to roar but no sound came out. The boy didn't even wake up!

4 When Sulley came back out, he was holding his throat and the scare canister was empty. "I've lost my roar," Sulley whispered to Mike.

5 Mike and Sulley went outside to discuss the problem. "If I can't roar, I can't scare!" Sulley croaked. Mike tried to think of a way to help Sulley.

6 Just then, Mike leaned back against the wall. "Arrrgh, that is so cold!" he screamed with shock, as shivers ran down his spine. He'd touched a freezing icicle!

7 Mike's scream gave Sulley an idea and he grinned at his friend. "I think we just found a frozen roar!" whispered Sulley, snapping off the icicle.

8 Mike and Sulley rushed back to their scare station. Sulley dashed through the door and heard the boy snoring. "Here goes," he chuckled.

When Sulley touched the boy's foot with the icicle, the boy screamed with shock. "Your frozen roar has done the trick, Sulley!" cheered Mike.

The End

About the Story ▶

1 What did Mike throw at Sulley?

2 What happened when Sulley tried to roar?

3 Who leaned against a wall and touched an icicle?

4 What happened when Sulley touched the boy's foot with an icicle?

Answers on page 67.

Sulley and Mike

Add some scary colours to this picture of the monsters at work.

Look
Which character is wearing a hat?

Answer on page 67.

27

Monster Changes

The Monsters, Inc. factory is very busy. Can you spot five changes in picture b?

a

b

Colour
Colour an eye each time you spot a difference.

28

Shady Scarers

See how quickly you can solve this monster puzzle.

a

b

c

d

Can you help Boo match each of these monsters to their shadows?

Mr Waternoose **Randall** **Mike** **Sulley**

Answers on page 67.

29

Puzzle Mania

The monsters need your help to solve these tricky teasers.

Monster Motors ▶

Can you draw lines to match each monster to its car?

a

b

c

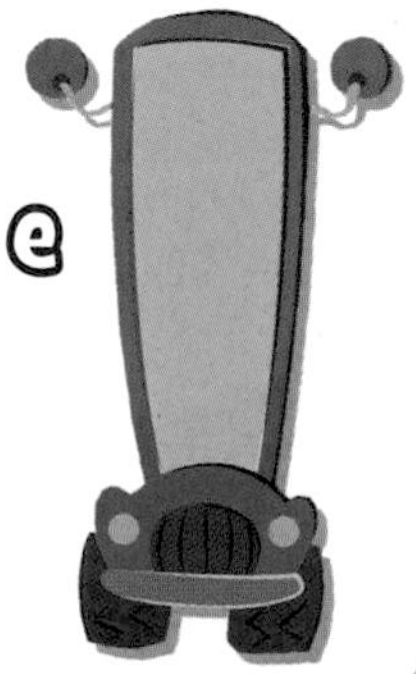

d

e

1

2

3

5

4

30

Tell the Time ▶

We've done the first one for you!

The monsters have had a busy day. Can you draw the little hand on each clock so that it shows the right time?

At 8 o'clock the monsters went to work.

At 1 o'clock the monsters had lunch.

At 7 o'clock Sulley collected a scream.

At 9 o'clock the monsters went ice-skating.

Spot

Can you see a pink sock in one of the pictures?

31

Answers on page 67.

Scary Fun!

Join Mike and Sulley on the scare floor to help solve these monster puzzles.

Puzzle Pieces ▶

Can you fit the jigsaw pieces into the gaps to complete this picture of Mike and Sulley?

Under the Sea

Let's search the bottom of the ocean to find out more about Nemo and his friends.

◄ Nemo

This little clownfish is brave and adventurous. He loves exploring and discovering new things.

◊ Sheldon

Nemo's best friend is allergic to water ... it makes him sneeze!

Marlin ►

Nemo's dad Marlin is a bit of a worrier. He tries to protect his only son from danger.

Disney · PIXAR
FINDING NEMO

♥ Crush and Squirt ♥

Laid-back turtles, Crush and Squirt, love to ride the East Australian Current.

🔹 Bruce

Shark Bruce isn't as scary as he looks. His motto is, 'fish are friends, not food'!

Colour
Colour the star next to your favourite character.

Dory ▶

Cheerful Dory has a terrible memory. She forgets things as soon as they've happened!

Dory the Teacher

Oh, dear! How can Dory teach Nemo's class when she can't even remember anyone's name?

One morning, Nemo's class were swimming around the playground as they waited for their school teacher, Mr. Ray, to arrive.

But Mr. Ray was very late that day! "He's not usually late …" Nemo thought, starting to worry.

Just then, Nemo's friend, Dory, swam into the playground and clapped her fins together to get everyone's attention. "Mr. Ray is not feeling very well and will be taking the week off to recover," Dory said. "So, I'll be your teacher instead!"

When Nemo asked why Dory was so late, she laughed. "I couldn't remember where I was going!"

she told him. Dory was the most forgetful fish that Nemo had ever met!

Soon, Dory was teaching the class about jellyfish and everything seemed to be going really well …

But Dory could not remember the names of Nemo's classmates. She called Sheldon 'Stephen' and then she called him 'Sabrina'. Dory called Pearl 'Pongo', Tad 'Mad' and she even called Nemo 'Elmo'!

That evening, Nemo told his dad about his day at school. "Dory's hopeless," Nemo groaned. "We hardly learnt anything because she kept getting everyone's name wrong and confusing us."

▲ Dory

▲ Nemo

"Well," Marlin said, with a smile, "perhaps there's something you can do to help Dory remember tomorrow."

Nemo scratched his head with his lucky fin as he thought about it. "I know!" Nemo laughed, as he had a great idea. "I'm going to make up a song to help Dory!"

And that's just what Nemo did. The song had a happy tune and it included the names of all of his classmates, with a little description of each of them. It went, "Sheldon's a seahorse, Nemo is orange with black and white stripes," and so on.

As soon as he was finished, Nemo swam to Dory's home in the reef and sang his cheerful song to her.

Dory loved it! "Songs are easy to remember, Nemo, who's orange with black and white stripes!" Dory sang.

The next day, Dory got everyone's name right every single time! She decided to teach the class Nemo's cheerful song.

When they had learnt all the words, Dory had a special treat. "Now, I'm going to teach you how to sing the song in whale!" And then Dory began to sing, making some very strange noises!

The End ⬤

Tad ▼

▼ Sheldon

⬤ Pearl

37

Fish Friends

Nemo is swimming with his friends. Can you draw lines to match the fish into pairs?

Count
How many fish are there are on this page?

a

b

c

d

e

f

g

h

Answers on page 68.

Mystery Object

Nemo and his friends have made a cool discovery!

Colour
Add some colour to the scene.

Ocean Trail

Can you help Marlin and Dory find Nemo? Follow the trail, answering the questions on the way.

Start ▶

3 Can you find this fish? Tick the box when you spot it.

1 How many turtles can you count?

2 What sound is this angry crab making?

snap

40

a **b**

c **d**

5 Circle the smallest starfish!

e

4 Trace the shape that the silver shoal has formed!

6 Say hello to Nemo!

⬥ Finish

41

Underwater Fun

Make a splash as you solve these exciting ocean activities.

Treasure Time ▶

What have Nemo and his friends found? Read the word in the bubbles to find out.

P

e

a

r

l

Write
Write the answer in the bubbles below!

42

Ocean Colouring ▷

Join the dots to complete
Sheldon, then colour the picture.

Spot
Who is hiding
in the coral?

Starfish Sizes ▷

Can you put these starfish
in order of size, starting
with the smallest?

a
b
c
d

43

Answers on page 68.

Toy Time

It's always playtime at Sunnyside! Download these fun facts about your favourite toys.

♥ Woody

Woody is the leader of the toys. He's a sensible, caring cowboy who always looks out for his friends.

Mr. Potato Head ◊

Mr. Potato Head makes the toys laugh. He's always losing his parts, which makes him look funny, too!

Toy Story 3

Buzz Lightyear ▷

Space Ranger Buzz loves adventure. He's very brave and likes to protect the other toys.

◁ Lotso

Lotso is in charge at Sunnyside Daycare Centre. But as the others soon realise, this cuddly bear isn't as nice as he looks.

Colour
Colour the star next to your favourite character.

Rex

Dinosaur Rex may look fierce, but he's actually scared of most things! He's very kind and caring.

Jessie △

Cowgirl Jessie is full of energy. Her favourite word is 'yee-ha'!

Hide it from Hamm

1 One day, Hamm was pretending to be Evil Dr. Porkchop. Woody and Buzz were trying to stop Hamm from discovering their top secret formula.

"I'll close my eyes and count to ten, but I'll find the secret formula no matter what!" cackled Hamm. The toys ran off so Hamm wouldn't hear them.

2 Woody quickly hid the formula under the rug. "Hamm will never find it there," giggled Jessie. "8 ... 9 ... 10! Coming ready or not!" yelled Hamm.

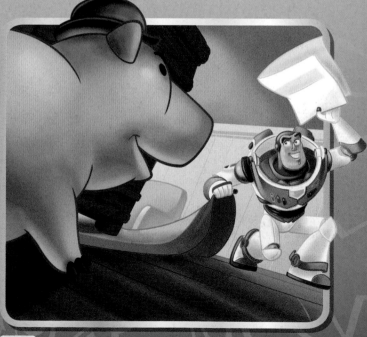

3 Hamm opened his eyes and began to snuffle. He headed straight for the rug. "Nothing escapes my super snout." Buzz quickly grabbed the formula.

Point to the biggest flower!

4 "Try and hide the formula again, but I'll find it!" sniggered Hamm. While he counted, the other toys searched for a better hiding place.

5 The toys were sure Hamm wouldn't look behind the clock. But they were wrong! "Tic-toc, tic-toc, I smell a formula behind a clock!" chuckled Hamm.

6 Hamm's super snout always sniffed it out. "OK, give us one last chance. If you find the formula again, you win the game!" said Woody.

7 This time, when Hamm opened his eyes and sniffed, he began to race around the room wildly. "I can smell it, but it keeps moving!" he wailed.

47

8 "You already had it!" laughed Woody. "We put it into your slot when you had your eyes closed." Hamm couldn't believe it.

9 He popped his cork and there was the formula! Hamm chuckled loudly with the other toys - he hadn't thought to look inside himself!

About the Story ▶

The End

Follow ▷

1 Who was Hamm pretending to be?

2 What were the other toys trying to hide from Hamm?

3 Where did Woody first hide the secret formula?

4 Why was Hamm so good at finding the formula?

5 How did the other toys finally trick Hamm?

48

Answers on page 68.

Cowboy Colouring

Woody, Bullseye and Jessie are horsing around!

Colour
Use your pens to complete the picture.

Toy Teasers

Can you help the toys complete the activities before Lotso finds them?

Cowboy Picture ▶

Which jigsaw piece isn't taken from this picture of Woody?

a

b

c

Rescue Mission ▷

Slinky is stuck in Lotso's trap! Which character will make it through the maze to save him?

Buzz Lightyear

Finish ▷

Mr. Potato Head

Hamm

Alien Activity ▷

Can you put these aliens in size order starting with the smallest?

Smallest

Largest

a

b

c

Answers on page 68.

51

Puzzle Fun

How quickly can you help the toys solve these brilliant puzzles?

Name Search ▶

Which four toy names can you find in this word wheel?

Word wheel letters: EYEWOODYBUZZZLOTSOBULLSEYE

Odd One Out ▶

Can you point to the odd one out in each row?

1
a   b   c

2
a   b   c

Answers on page 68.

Rope Trails

Who has Jessie caught with her lasso?

Start ▶

Follow
Use your finger to follow the trails.

Rex

Buzz

Slinky

Answer on page 68.

In a Muddle!

Yee-ha! Jessie is calling for your help with these activities.

Perfect Match ▶

Only one ball matches the one on the right. Can you spot it?

a

b

c

d

e

54

Toy Changes ▶

Some of Mr. and Mrs. Potato Head's parts have changed! There are five differences in picture b. Can you spot them all?

a

b

Colour
Colour a part when you find a difference.

Find the Friend ▶

Cross off all the letters that appear more than once in the grid below to find out the name of a toy friend.

S	M	L	J	I
H	E	A	H	O
J	N	M	H	K
A	O	Y	M	E

Answers on page 68.

55

It's Playtime!

The toys are playing at Sunnyside. Join in the fun by answering the questions.

1

Who is wearing a hat?
Write your answer below.

....

2 Is Buzz running or sitting?

3 Colour a star each time you spot an alien.

4 Who is riding through the air on a spinning top?

Meet the 'Bots

It's the year 2805 and planet Earth is covered in rubbish. Scroll down to find out more ...

WALL·E ▽

WALL·E collects rubbish and crushes it into cubes. As the only robot left on Earth, he's a little lonely ... until probe-bot EVE comes along.

Eve ▷

EVE is a sleek probe-bot. She's sent from space to search Earth for signs of life. EVE is unsure of WALL·E at first, but they soon become best friends.

Cockroach ▷

WALL·E's pet cockroach is his only friend on Earth. He is very loyal and is always by WALL·E's side.

Disney · PIXAR

WALL·E

Odd One Out ▷

Which robot is the odd one out?
Click on the correct robot by
colouring the arrow next to it.

a   b   c

◁ **M-O**

M-O works on
board the Axiom,
where all the
humans now live.
His job is to keep
the star liner nice
and clean.

Colour
Colour the star
next to your
favourite
character.

Answer on page 68.

The Big Bounce

One day 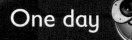 was gathering rubbish ready

to crush into s, when he saw a shiny .

didn't know what to do with the

so he tried to find , hoping that she would

know what to do. But was a long way

away, there were lots of s to travel

around and the was heavy. As

rushed to reach , he dropped the .

60

The  bounced and that gave

a brilliant idea! He attached

the to his tracks and bounced

over the s in no time! When

saw , she laughed

with her loudest robot beep!

took off the so that

could have a go.

and spent the rest

of the day bouncing over the s

until the sun went down and it was

time for bed!

The End ▶

61

Space Puzzles

Join WALL·E and EVE in space to complete these fun activities.

Robot Words ▷

Can you find the words below in the wordsearch? They go across and down.

M	S	T	A	R	B
D	E	P	X	O	L
J	S	P	A	C	E
E	I	W	L	K	O
P	L	A	N	E	T
S	R	O	S	T	F

STAR   PLANET   SPACE   ROCKET

62

Cube Maze ▶

WALL·E is searching for the plant. Can you help him reach it through the maze by stepping on only the ▢ cubes?

▼ Start

Finish ▲

Answers on page 68.

63

Adventure Time

WALL·E needs your help to solve these space teasers.

Count

How many yellow stars can you count below?

Picture Puzzle ▶

Can you put the sections on the right into the correct order? Then, copy the letters, to see what WALL·E is thinking about.

c
s
b
u
e

WALL·E

_ _ _ _ _

Write your answer here.

Answer on page 68.

Robot Clean-up ▶

WALL·E is hard at work collecting rubbish.

Colour
Finish this picture with your brightest pens.

65

Robot Fun

Help WALL-E match these robots into pairs. Which one doesn't have a match?

a

b

c

d

e

f

g

h

i

WALL-E

Answers on page 68.

Answers

Pages 14-15

Car-azy Puzzles!
Top Secret: Mater.
Picture Puzzle:
Lightning.
Odd One Out: a.

Page 16

I-Spy ...
a – Lightning, b – Holley,
c – Professor Z, d – Finn.

Page 17

Crack the Code
London.

Pages 18-19

World Winner
Lightning – 10.
Francesco – 8.
Max – 8.
Raoul – 9.
Lightning is the winner.
Car Clues: Fillmore.

Page 20

Race Time

Page 21

Car Search

Page 26

About the Story
1. A snowball.
2. No sound came out.
3. Mike.
4. He screamed with shock.

Page 27

Sulley and Mike
Mike is wearing a hat.

Page 28

Monster Changes

Page 29

Shady Scarers
Mr Waternoose – d,
Randall – c, Mike – a,
Sulley – b.

Pages 30-31

Puzzle Mania
Monster Motors: 1 – d,
2 – b, 3 – e, 4 – a, 5 – c.
Tell the Time:

The pink sock is
in picture 2.

Pages 32-33

Scary Fun!
Puzzle Pieces: 1 – b,
2 – e, 3 – a, 4 – d, 5 – c.
Monster Maze:

There are 7 scream
canisters.